INTRO TO YOUR ENVIRONMENT

Oliver S. Owen

Published by Abdo & Daughters, 4940 Viking Dr., Suite 622, Edina, Minnesota 55435.

Library bound edition distributed by Rockbottom Books, Pentagon Tower, P.O. Box 36036, Minneapolis, Minnesota 55435.

Illustrated by Kristen Copham   Edited by Bob Italia

Cover Photo: Stock Market
Inside Photos: Stock Market-pgs. 14, 15, 16, 20, 23, 33
                Peter Arnaold-pgs. 10, 17, 34
                All stock-pgs. 12, 27

Library of Congress Cataloging-in-Publication Data

Owen, Oliver S., 1949-
    Intro to Your Environment / written by Oliver S. Owen; [edited by Bob Italia].
        p.   cm -- (Target earth)
    Includes bibliographical references and index.
    Summary: Describes the ecology of four environments--the land, fresh water, ocean, and atmosphere--and gives exercises in nature observation.
    ISBN 1-56239-204-2
    1. Ecology--Juvenile literature. 2. Ecology--United States--Juvenile literature.
[1. Ecology.] I. Italia, Robert, 1955-
II. Title. III. Series.
QH541. 14. 095   1993
574.5--dc20   93-7746
                                                          CIP
                                                           AC

About the Author

Oliver S. Owen is a Professor Emeritus for the University of Wisconsin at Eau Claire. He is the co-author of *Natural Resource Conservation: An Ecological Approach* (Macmillan, 1991). Dr. Owen has a Ph.D. in Zoology from Cornell University.

The Target Earth™ Earthmobile Scientific Advisory Board

 Thanks to the trees from which this recycled paper was first made.

Chapter 1–How Your Environment is Organized 5

- Population..5
- Community...6
- Ecosystem..6
- Ecosphere 8

Chapter 2–Your Land Environment: The Biomes........................9

- The Tundra 9
- Animals of the Tundra..10
- The Northern Coniferous Forest...11
- The Deciduous Forest...13
- The Grasslands 13
- The Desert 14
- The Tropical Rainforest..16

Chapter 3–Your Fresh Water Environment...............................19

- Lakes 20
- Rivers 22
- Animals of the Lakes and Rivers 22
- Fresh Water Wetlands...23
- Animals of the Wetlands 24

Chapter 4–Your Marine Environment 25

- The Shallows 26
- The Abyss 26
- The Ocean Bottom 27
- Coral Reefs 28
- Barrier Islands 28
- Estuaries 30
- Salt Water Wetlands 30

Chapter 5–Your Atmosphere's Environment 31

- Animals of the Air 34
- How Your Environments are Tied Together 36
- Why We Should Take Care of Our Environments 37

Glossary 37

Projects 39

Index 44

Chapter 1

How Your Environment is Organized

Your body has several levels of organization. We can list them from the lowest to the highest level:

- atom
- molecule
- cell
- tissue
- organ
- organ system
- you–the organism!

The environment around us also has levels of organization:

- population
- community
- ecosystem
- ecosphere

Population

Population usually refers to the total number of people living in a given area. For example, the population of Minneapolis is 368,000. Minnesota's population is 4,375,00. In this book, population will indicate the total number of any kind of organism, plant or animal, living in a given area. We might speak of the population of grizzly bears in Glacier National Park, the population of robins in your backyard, or even the population of fleas on your dog!

Community

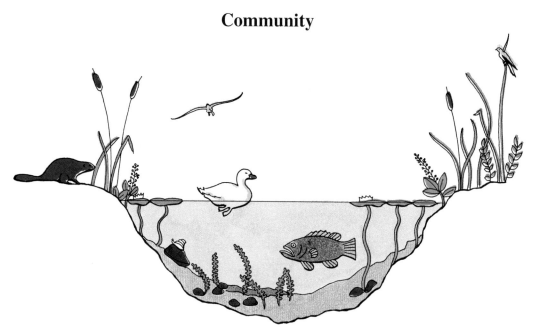

Fish, birds, mammals, and plants make up a community.

Community

Until now, you have used *community* to refer to a village, town or city. In this book, community will refer to all the organisms, human and non-human, living in a certain place. For example, the community in your backyard probably includes robins, elms, oaks, rose bushes, tulips, earthworms, ants, grasshoppers, butterflies, mice, rabbits, and maybe even some mosquitos, ticks and poison ivy! And we can't overlook the billions of bacteria that live in the soil, water and air!

Ecosystem

Ecosystem is a shortened version of ecological system. An ecosystem may be defined as a group of organisms that interact with each other and their environment in a self-perpetuating system.

You do not live in isolation. Every second of your life, from the cradle to the present, you have been interacting with other living organisms, and with your non-living environment.

Ecosystem

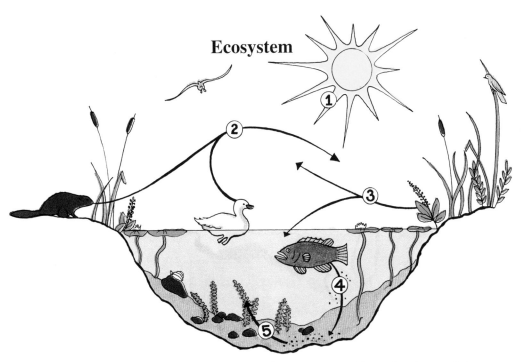

An ecosystem is made up of a community that interacts with each other and the environment. Plants interact with solar energy (1) to form oxygen (3) that animals breathe. Animals exhale carbon dioxide (2) that plants absorb to make food. Waste from animals (4) form nutrients (5) that plants also use for food.

Take a deep breath. The oxygen you are inhaling was released from the leaves of green plant–maybe even from the leaves of the grass, shrubs and trees that you can see from your classroom or home. Those trees also provide nesting sites for birds. These birds may feed on the bugs that feed on the leaves of the trees.

What did you eat for lunch? A ham sandwich? The bread in that sandwich was probably made from wheat. The wheat plants give off oxygen, which could be used by the bugs which feed on the wheat. The bugs serve as food for birds and shrews. The wheat plants depend for their survival on the farmers who cultivate and fertilize the soil before sowing wheat seeds. The ham in your sandwich was derived from a pig. This pig ate many kinds of foods: corn, rats, mice, bugs, and even garbage! The pig's gut served as a "home" for parasites like tapeworms, hookworms and roundworms.

"OK," you say. "I understand that I interact directly or indirectly with many other organisms. But how does the non-living matter around me affect my survival?"

For one thing, if you stopped breathing oxygen, your life would come to a sudden end. And how about the minerals in the soil? Take iron, for example. Your body needs this element to produce hemoglobin, the red pigment in each of your body's 25 trillion red blood cells.

Take another non-living part of your environment–air temperature. Of all the planets that orbit around the sun, only Earth has a temperature that permits your survival, and that of all other organisms. And how about water? You are 80 percent water! You would not be able to survive for more than two weeks without a drink of water!

Ecosphere

All the Earth's ecosystems are inter-connected to form one global ecosystem. That portion of the Earth which is occupied by this global ecosystem is known as the ecosphere. It extends from seven miles (12km) below the surface of the deepest oceans to mountain peaks more than five miles high (8km). If the Earth were the size of an apple, the ecosphere would be thinner than the peeling!

Chapter 2

Your Land Environment: the Biomes

Has your family ever driven from Maine to California? Perhaps not. But it would be an exciting trip–at least from an ecological viewpoint. You would see dramatic changes in the landscape as you sped along the highways . You would see the evergreen forests of Maine and the beech-maple woodlands of Ohio. You would see the wind-swept Kansas prairies and the cactus deserts of Arizona. Each of these regions is a biome (BYE-ome).

A biome is the largest land community which biologists easily recognize. A biome is the biological result of the interaction of climate, soil, water and organisms. There are many kinds of biomes.

Tundra

The Siberian word tundra (TUN-dra) means "north of the timberline." The term is highly appropriate because a tundra stretches from the edge of the forests northward to the belt of constant ice and snow. The tundra moved northward in the wake of the melting glaciers about 10,000 years ago.

The tundra extends around the globe in the far northern latitudes. During June and July, the northern tundra is the "land of the midnight sun" because the sun never sets. But in midwinter, it becomes a "land of mid-day darkness" because the sun never rises! That's because in summer the tundra portion of planet Earth faces the sun. In winter, it faces away from the sun.

The frozen tundra in the Northwest Territory, Canada.

Annual rainfall in the tundra is less than 10 inches (25 cm) per year. Vegetation is sparse because of the cold weather and the short six-week growing season. Son the tundra is sometimes called an Arctic desert.

Much of the sub-soil is frozen year round. This layer is called the perma-frost. Dwarf willows are common plants. Although only a few feet tall, they may be well over a century old! Other characteristic plants are sedges, grasses, moss, huckleberries, crowberries, and dwarf birches.

Animals of the Tundra

To survive the sub-zero cold of the tundra, birds are well-insulated with a dense covering of feathers. Mammals have a thick layer of fur. Both birds and mammals have a thick layer of fat under the skin. Small mammals, like lemmings, mice, and rabbits, escape the cold by burrowing under the snow. Cold-blooded animals like frogs, lizards, and snakes are absent because they cannot cope with the low temperatures.

In spring and summer, the thousands of lakes and shallow ponds swarm with insects like deerflies, blackflies, and mosquitos. They serve as food for dense flocks of migratory waterfowl that arrive from the south. The musk ox is the only large herbivore (HER-bih-vore) or "plant-eater" to remain in the tundra all year. The caribou (reindeer) stay only during the summer. The remainder of the year, they spend in the coniferous forest biome to the south. The ptarmigan is a characteristic resident of the tundra. It is a grouse-like ground bird which changes color with the season in order to escape predation by foxes, wolves, and the snowy owl.

The Biomes

Biome	Climate	Common Plants	Common Animals
Tundra	-57°–16°C	Lichens, mosses, dwarf willows	Ptarmigan, snowy owl, lemming, caribou, musk ox, Arctic fox
Coniferous forest	-54°–21°C	Black spruce, white spruce, balsam fir, white birch, aspen	Spruce budworm, tussock moth, moose, snoeshoe hare, lynx
Deciduous forest	-30°–38°C	Oak, hickory, beech maple, black walnut, yellow poplar	White-tailed deer, gray squirrel, skunk, opossum, black beer
Grassland	40°–60°C	Little and big bluetem, grama grass, buffalo grass	Meadowlark, burrowing owl, pronghorned antelope, badger, jackrabbit, coyote
Desert	2°–47°C	Prickly pear cactus, saguaro cactus, creosote bush, mesquite, sagebrush	Diamond-backed rattlesnake, Gila monster, roadrunner kangaroo rat, wild pig
Savannah	13°–40°C	Baobab tree, acacia tree, grasses	Zebra, giraffe, wildebeest, elephant antelope
Tropical rainforest	18°–35°C	Many species	Many species

Northern Coniferous Forest

The northern coniferous (con-IF-er-us) or "cone-bearing" forest is composed of evergreen, and needle-leaved trees like spruce, fir, and pine. This biome forms a broad band just south of the tundra in North America, Europe, and Asia. The forest floor is covered with a dense carpet of needles. The flexibility of the branches enable them to support a heavy layer of snow without breaking.

Among the herbivores are the caribou, moose, elk, mule deer, porcupine, squirrel, chipmunk, and mice. Characteristic carnivores or "meat-eaters" include the grizzly bear, timber wolf, fox, and lynx. Outbreaks of insect pests like pine beetles and spruce budworms provide food for migratory birds (warblers, thrushes, and woodpeckers) that come from the south in spring.

A coniferous or "cone-bearing" forest is composed of evergreen, and needle-leaved trees like spruce, fir, and pine. This coniferous forest is in Baxter State Park, Maine.

The coniferous forest biome has an annual rainfall of 15-40 inches (37 to 100 cm). Average temperatures range from 20 degrees Fahrenheit (-6.6 degrees Celsius) in winter to 70 degrees Fahrenheit (21 degrees Celsius) in summer. This biome has a 150-day growing season.

The Biomes

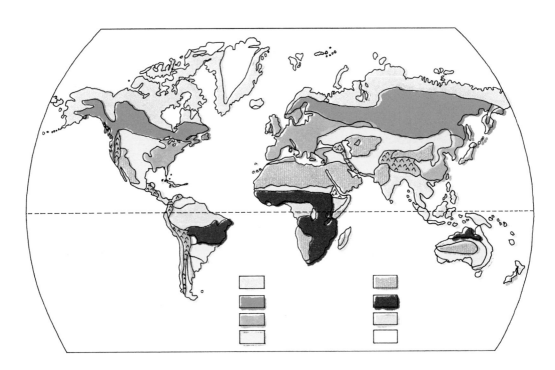

The Deciduous Forest

The deciduous (deh-SID-u-us) trees are not evergreen. They lose their leaves in autumn. In the United States, this biome occurs mainly east of the Mississippi River and south of the coniferous forest biome.

Before the white settlers came from Europe, the deciduous forest was almost unbroken. But today, settlements, farming, logging, mining and road construction has reduced the forest to only .1 percent of its original area!

The deciduous forest biome has abundant rainfall–at least 30 inches (75 cm) per year. It also has a long growing season. Plant growth is the greatest of any North American biome except the tropical rainforest in Puerto Rico. Common trees are oak, hickory and maple.

Much of the vegetation in the deciduous forest provides food (tender twigs, leaves, acorns, hickory nuts, chestnuts, maple seeds, raspberries, and blackberries), nesting and breeding sites, as well as protection from storms for a great variety of animals. Among characteristic herbivores are deer, squirrels, chipmunks, rabbits, and grouse. Raccoons and opossums are prominent omnivores–they eat both plants and animals. The black bear, fox, shrews, hawks, eagles, and owls are typical carnivores.

The Grasslands

Major grasslands or prairies occur in two regions in the United States. One area extends from the eastern slopes of the Rockies to the Mississippi River. The other is in the more moist areas between the Sierra Mountains on the west and the Rockies to the east. Annual rainfall is between 10 and 30 inches (25 to 75 cm) per year. Dominant plants include big bluestem grass, little bluestem grass, buffalo grass and grama grass.

The grass plants have long branching root systems which extend several feet into the soil. A grass only 15 inches (37.5 cm) tall may have over 100 miles (166 km) of roots. With such root systems, grasses are able to get water even during severe drought.

Grassland soils are very fertile. Almost 99 percent of the original American grassland biome has been converted to farms that are growing corn, wheat, and soybeans, or are pig "factories."

Grasslands or prairies occur in two regions in the United States. One area extends from the eastern slopes of the Rockies to the Mississippi River. The other is between the Sierra Mountains on the west and the Rockies on the east.

Grassland animals have certain traits. Many are excellent hoppers or jumpers. With their strong hind legs, many grassland animals such as grasshoppers, jumping mice, and jackrabbits are able to rise above the dense grasses in order to see ahead. Because of the lack of trees from which they might sing, many grassland birds, such as the lark, sing while in flight in order to attract mates. Characteristic herbivores are pronghorn antelope, jackrabbits, prairie dogs, mice, and grasshoppers. Ranchers have replaced the buffalo of the past with beef cattle. Prominent carnivores are the coyote and badger. The grasslands of Africa support herbivores such as zebra, antelope, and giraffes. Lions, leopards, and cheetahs prey upon these animals.

The Desert

The world's deserts are located primarily in the United States, Mexico, Chile, Africa (Sahara), Asia (Gobi) and Australia. America's deserts are located mainly in the hotter, drier parts of California, New Mexico, Arizona, Texas, Nevada, Idaho, Utah and Oregon. Annual rainfall is less than ten inches (25 cm). But rain may fall as cloudbursts that cause flash floods and severe soil erosion.

America's deserts are located in the hotter, drier southwestern part of the United States. Annual rainfall is less than ten inches (25 cm) and temperatures range from 50 degrees Fahrenheit (10°C) at night to 120 degrees Fahrenheit (49°C) during the day.

Summer temperatures range from about 50 degrees Fahrenheit (10 Celsius) at night to about 120 degrees Fahrenheit (49 Celsius) during the day. The author has recorded summer temperature on the desert floor in Texas that reached 140 degrees Fahrenheit (60 Celsius)! Only plants and animals that are adapted to withstand extreme heat and drought can survive.

A rattlesnake, found in southwestern United States and Central and South American.

A variety of cacti, such as the barrel cactus and the prickly pear cactus, grow in the desert. One cactus, the century plant, grows to a height of 50 feet (16 m) and lives to be 100 years old. It serves as nesting sites for woodpeckers and owls. Other prominent desert plants are greasewood, creosote bush, and mesquite. Many kinds of wild flowers burst into bloom after a sudden thundershower–causing the desert to blaze with color.

Characteristic herbivores are pocket mice, kangaroo rates, jackrabbits, and wild pigs. The kangaroo rat conserves water by producing solid urine. Both the mice and rats escape heat by remaining in burrows during the day and coming out at night. Prominent meat-eaters are the rattlesnakes, gila (HEE-la) monster (lizard), and the desert fox.

The Tropical Rainforest

Tropical rainforests are found in Central America, South America, Africa and Southeast Asia. They cover an area equal to the United States. Heavy rains may occur daily through much of the year. A rainforest needs at least eighty inches (200 cm) of rain annually to develop. The thick crowns of the trees screen out much of the sunlight, so the forest floor is dark. Optimists call the rainforest a "green cathedral." Pessimists call it a "humid hell."

The tropical rainforests have a rich variety of plants and animals. There may be more species of organisms living in a single tree than in the entire coniferous forest biome!

Tropical rainforests have a rich variety of plants and animals. Tropical rainforests provide wildlife habitat to 75 percent of the Earth's organisms.

The tropical rainforests have many functions. Besides providing wildlife habitat to 75 percent of the Earth's organisms, the rainforests also:

- provide a home to 200 million people
- control soil erosion by protecting the Earth from wind and water
- serve as a living sponge by soaking up rainfall and later releasing it to farmers so they can grow food for one billion people
- provide a habitat for plants from which cancer-fighting drugs can be derived
- absorb thousands of tons of carbon dioxide from the air and help control a harmful warm-up of the Earth's climate

Snakes are varied and abundant. One kind, the palm viper, hangs in the vines and bushes and catches birds as they pass by. It then injects its deadly venom. At least 369 kinds of birds have been identified on only five acres (.0046k) of tropical rainforest in Costa Rica–more than in all of Alaska! One species, known as the scythebill, uses its long red bill to probe for insects. Parrots are numerous.

The fish-eating bat catches its prey at night. The Brazilian long-nosed bat lives in tree cavities. Howler monkeys and spider monkeys are prominent. The ocelot or "leopard cat," hunts at night and preys on mice, wood rats, rabbits, snakes, lizards, birds, monkeys, and deer.

Some insects are huge. The wing span of one South American moth is almost 12 inches (30.5 cm). Up to 600 kinds of butterflies can be found in the rainforests of just one tropical island–as many species as can be found in the entire United States. Some spiders along the Amazon River in South America are large enough to feed on birds caught in their webs!

Chapter 3
Your Fresh Water Environment

There are three kinds of fresh water habitats on Earth: lakes, rivers, and wetlands. One or more of these habitats serve humans by providing:

- sport and commercial fisheries
- recreational opportunities such as fishing, hunting, swimming and boating
- food, cover and breeding sites for wildlife
- scenic beauty
- moderate climate

Lakes

Many thousands of lakes dot America's landscape. The combined states of Minnesota and Wisconsin have at least 30,000. Many northern lakes originated as melt waters from glaciers. The Great Lakes, which contain 20 percent of the world's fresh water supply, were formed the same way. Other lakes, like beautiful Crater Lake in Oregon, may form when rain water fills up the craters of extinct volcanos.

During this century, many artificial lakes known as reservoirs (REZ-er-vors) were formed when dams were built across a river. A good example as the Hoover Dam on the Colorado River, located on the border between Arizona and Nevada. This dam is more than 44 stories high and has enough cement in it to pave a two-lane highway from coast to coast! The dam's generators provide electricity for many cities in the Southwest. Water from Lake Mead, which formed behind the dam, is used to irrigate more than one million acres of farmland. Lake Mead also provides water for several cities in California.

Hydroelectric System

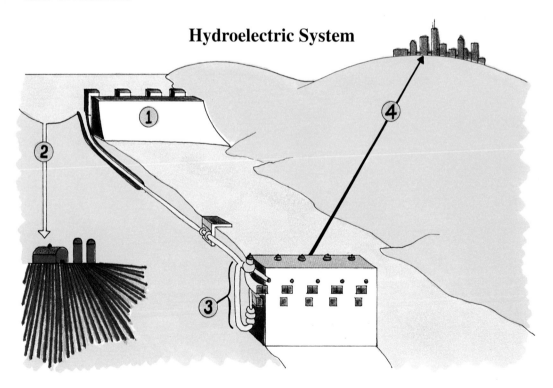

Adam (1) forms a lake from which water is used for irrigating farm crops (2). Water flows to a power plant and passes through a water turbine (3) that drives an electrical generator. The electricity is used by nearby towns and cities (4).

Photosynthesis

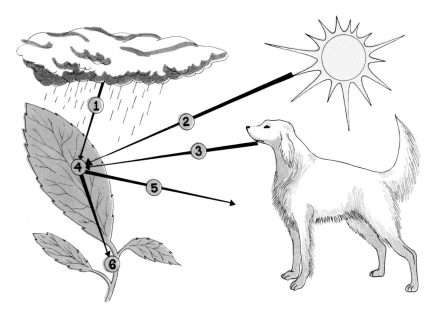

Water from a rain cloud (1), energy from sunlight (2), and carbon dioxide from an animal (3) are absorbed by a plant (4) to make oxygen (5) and food (6).

Large lakes have a moderating influence on climate. The famous fruit-growing region along the eastern shore of Lake Michigan depends on air blowing eastwards of the lake. This air prevents early frost damage and extends the growing season.

Unlike rivers, the water temperature in many larger and deeper lakes becomes layered or stratified (STRAT-ih-fied) during much of the year. This determines the distribution of fish and other organisms. Most of the lake's dissolved oxygen comes from the photosynthetic (foe-toe-sin-THEH-tic) activity of both rooted plants like water lilies and floating plants like green algae.

Lake Tenaya in Yosemite National Park.

Rivers

Some rivers have had their beginning in the melt waters of glaciers that existed 10,000 or more years ago. Other arose from water that bubbled to the surface from underground springs. The United States has thousands of rivers and streams. The three largest rivers are the Mississippi River is 2,347 miles long (3,776 km)–the third longest in the entire world! The mud carried by the lower Mississippi forms one of the most fertile valleys on Earth.

There are several important differences between lake and river ecosystems. Unlike many lakes, rivers are usually well aerated (oxygen levels are high). This is due to the flow of the water, and the somewhat large amount of water exposed to the air. Photosynthesis is not as important a source of oxygen as in a lake. Unlike a lake, the river is an open ecosystem in which energy-supplying materials are constantly being supplied from the land on each side.

In autumn, thousands of leaves may fall into the water. The river also may be enriched by plant stems, nuts, seeds, weeds, flowers, cow manure, commercial fertilizer, and the bodies of worms, insects and mice that are washed into the river during a flood.

Animals of the Lakes and Rivers

Many millions of microscopic "water fleas" swarm in the world's lakes and rivers. These tiny organisms are called crustaceans (crus-STAY-shunz) and serve as fish food. If you wade in the shallow water near shore, you can find a great variety of animals–from the crayfish that tickle your toes to snails, tadpoles, turtles and minnows. If you pick up a rock from the bottom and look at it closely, you might find the young stages or larvae (LAR-vey) of insects such as dragon flies or may flies.

More than 7,000 kinds of fish live in lakes and streams around the world. There are at least 2,000 species of catfish alone living in Africa, Asia and South America. For thousands of years, humans have "gone fishing"–either for much-needed food, or just for fun. Even the Stone Age humans scooped fish from shallow pools with their bare hands! Egyptian tombs built 2,000 years before Christ show people netting fish from boats.

In North American waters, fish range in size from the rainbow darter, which is only three inches (7.5 cm) long, to the 16-foot (4.8 m) sturgeon! Many fish are very sensitive to water temperature. Trout and salmon prefer cold water while carp and bullheads like a warmer environment. Some fish even live in the hot spring of Yellowstone National Park where the water temperature gets up to 104 degrees Fahrenheit (40 degrees Centigrade)!

Common fish found in the lakes and streams of the United States are carp, bullheads, bass, perch, bluegill, walleye, pike, muskellunge, and trout. Pacific salmon have recently been introduced to the Great Lakes. Salmon, smelt and shad migrate from the ocean to fresh water streams to spawn. Eels do the reverse.

Fish serve as food for many kinds of animals. Among the fish-eaters are shordwelling raccoon, otter and mink. Long-legged wading birds like herons and egrets stalk fish in the shallows. Snapping turtles can make a quick meal out of a stringer of fish tied to a dock– as the author knows full well!

Out in the deeper water of a lake, birds like terns and fish hawks will dive from the air to seize shallow-swimming fish. Bald eagles and gulls scoop up dead fish that float on the surface. The loon is a spectacular bird on the northern lakes. It is a highly specialized fish-eater. It can dive to a depth of 100 feet (30.5 meters) and stay underwater for 10 minutes!

Fresh Water Wetlands

Bogs, marshes and swamps are all examples of wetlands. A wetland is land that is flooded at least part of the year. Some marshes begin as shallow lakes that gradually become filled with soil and decaying plants. The lower 48 states have about 90 million wetland acres. Alaska has twice that amount. The wetlands include the wet Arctic grasslands (tundra) of northern Canada, the prairie potholes of the northern Great Plains, the bottom land forests of the Southeast, the spruce and tamarack bogs of the northern states, and the cat-tail and bulrush marshes that occur in low-lying areas in much of the United States and Canada.

Wetlands have many functions:

- They regulate and store the flow of streams. This reduces flood damage.
- They control pollution of lake and streams by sediment and toxic chemicals.
- They provide areas where wild rice, blueberries and cranberries can be grown.
- They provide excellent habitat for many of our nation's threatened and endangered species of wildlife.

Bogs, marshes and swamps are all examples of wetlands.
A wetland is land that is flooded at least part of the year.

Animals of the Wetlands

The wetlands are so important to wildlife that the U.S. government has included 10 million acres (25,000 km) of them in the National Wildlife Refuge System. The most productive duck "factory" in North America is in the wetland fringes of tiny pothole lakes in Manitoba, Saskatchewan, Alberta, the Dakotas, western Minnesota and north-western Iowa. These wetlands and potholes provide all the basic needs of waterfowl, such as food, shelter from storms, refuge from predators, and good nesting sites.

The salt water marshes that border the Atlantic and Gulf Coasts provide winter homes for millions of water birds such as ducks, geese, swans and long-legged wading birds like herons, egrets and cranes. The winter home of the endangered Whooping Crane is in the Aransas Wildlife Refuge of coastal Texas.

Both salt water and fresh water wetlands serve as excellent habitat (living places) for a great variety of other animals. These include snails, crustaceans, frogs, muskrat, beaver, otter and mink.

Chapter 4

Your Marine Environment

Our planet "Earth" has the wrong name. It should really be called the "water" planet! After all, oceans cover more than 70 percent of it. The ocean basins were formed by movements of the Earth's crust about 200 million years ago. These basins gradually filled with water because of heavy rains that continued for thousands of years. The ocean water is about 3.5 percent salt. The salts came from the rocks that line the basin. Hundreds of tributary streams also wash salts into the ocean. (These salts help keep a swimmer afloat!)

There are five major oceans:

- Atlantic
- Pacific
- Indian
- Arctic
- Antarctic

The ocean waters are constantly moving around. Eventually, a single molecule of water (H_2O) moves through every one of our world's oceans. But it would take 5,000 years!

The ocean plays a very important role in your survival, other humans, and that of almost every living organism. It plays an important function in shaping the global climate. It re-distributes the warmth from sunshine through its ocean currents. One of these currents is the Gulf Stream which flows northward along the Atlantic Coast. (That's why President Clinton could address news reporters on the White House lawn in mid-February without wearing a coat!) Our oceans form a gigantic storehouse of life-giving oxygen. They also provide a habitat for more than 250,000 kinds of plants and animals. The global marine fish catch amounts to about 100 million tons (90 billion kg) every year.

The Shallows

The shallows is a region of water which overlies the shelf-like extension of the continental land mass known as the continental shelf. The shallows have a width of 10 to 200 miles (16 to 322 km) and a maximum depth of about 600 feet (183 m).

The water in the shallows is somewhat warm and rich in nutrients. Sunlight normally penetrates to the bottom. As a result, a considerable amount of photosynthesis takes place.

More than 90 percent of the commercial food fishes live in the shallows. They include salmon, cod, halibut, mackerel, sardines, herring, anchovy, red snapper, and tuna. Sharks also populate the shallows. They range in size from a 4-inch (10-cm) species that weighs only one ounce to the 60-foot (18-m) whale shark that weighs 15 tons (13,500 kg)–twice as much as an African elephant! Whales like the blue whale and the gray whale frequent the shallows. The gray whale makes regular migrations up and down the Pacific Coast and can be seen from shore with a good pair of binoculars. The blue whale is the largest animal that has ever lived on the planet! It may be twice the length of a boxcar–over 100 feet (30.5 m) and weigh over 100 tons (90,000 kg). The ocean shallows near the coast is also the favorite habitat of porpoises, sea otters, walruses, seals, and sea cows.

The Abyss

The abyss (uh-BISS) is the cold dark-water zone at the bottom of the ocean. It lies immediately above the ocean floor. The water is extremely cold–close to the freezing point. Sunlight cannot penetrate the abyss. Photosynthesis cannot take place here, so dissolved oxygen levels are very low.

Water pressures are very high–over a 1,000 pounds (450 kg) per square inch! This means that the column of water above one square inch of ocean bottom weighs more than 1,000 pounds (450 kg). Such pressure would quickly crush a human body. There may be an abundance of nutrient-rich sediments on the ocean floor. These nutrients were derived from the decaying bodies of marine organisms that drifted down from the sunlit waters far above.

Ocean Life Zones

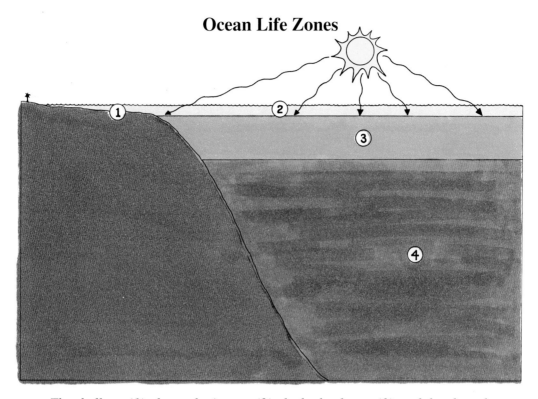

The shallows (1), the euphotic zone (2), the bathyal zone (3), and the abyssal zone (4). The Euphotic zone is sunlit, can support photosynthesis, and has a high oxygen level. The bathyal zone has little light and cannot support photosynthesis.

The abyss has some very unusual kinds of fish. Many have special organs that produce flashes of light. This enables them to find food and mates in the inky darkness. The deep sea angler fish has a terrifying look. It has sharp needle-like teeth and a huge mouth. But the angler is only three inches long (7.5 cm)! it lures smaller fish with a worm-like structure that dangles above its mouth.

The Ocean Bottom

Scientists once believed that the ocean bottom was perfectly flat and smooth. We now know this is not true, thanks to observations from diving bells and research submarines. Some of our planet's most spectacular scenery lies beneath the sea! If we could hike along the ocean bottom, we would see mountains, ridges, plains, plateaus and deep canyons. Such underwater landscapes are typical of the Atlantic Ocean bottom extending from Florida eastward to Spain.

Coral Reefs

Coral reefs often form in the shallow water zones of the tropical and sub-tropical oceans. They are largely made up of calcium carbonate secreted by small coral animals. They may be built on shallow continental shelves or on submerged volcanos. One-third of all species of marine fish live in, on or near coral reefs. The Great Barrier Reef off the northeast coast of Australia is the largest coral formation in the world. It is more than 1,250 miles (2,011 km) long.

Coral reefs have been called "gardens of the sea" because of their bright and varied colors. Thereds, greens, yellows, and blues are partly caused by the presence of many sea animals like mollusks, sea anemones, star fish, and fish.

Carnivorous fish with sharp needle-like teeth lie in ambush in the tiny caverns that honeycomb the reef and seize smaller fish as they swim by.

Barrier Islands

The barrier islands form a broken chain that skirts the Atlantic and Gulf Coasts of the United States from Maine to Texas. There are almost 300 of them. About 40 percent of them have been commercially developed. Among them are Cape Cod, Massachusetts; Atlantic City, New Jersey; Coney Island, New York; Cape Hatteras, North Carolina; and Miami Beach, Florida. Many islands that have not been developed are characterized by sand dunes and sea shells. The barrier beaches are well named. They form an important barrier to storm-whipped waves that could otherwise pound the coastal areas and cause serious erosion and property damage.

The islands are part of a river of sand that flows south along the Atlantic and Gulf coasts. There is a continual movement of these islands toward the mainland because of the action of winds, currents, and waves.

Vegetation is sparse. Typical plants are marsh grasses, pine, and oak. Common animals include mollusks, sand dollars, starfish, and insects. Thousands of shorebirds visit the sand flats during migration.

A shallow coral reef in Fiji.

Estuaries

All rivers sooner or later flow into the sea. The region where the fresh water of the river mixes with the salt water of the ocean is known as an estuary (ESS-tew-air-ee). An estuary is a partly enclosed portion of the ocean shallows. Land formations determine the estuary's size, shape, and water volume. The estuary represents a "hybrid" between the ocean and a river. They have some characteristics of each. But estuaries also have distinctive features all their own.

The water is a mixture of fresh water from the river and salt water from the ocean. The water level in the estuary rises and falls with the tides. Sixty percent of the marine fish harvested by Americans spend part of their life cycle in estuaries. Many marine fish use the estuary as a nursery in which they spend the early stage of their life.

America's largest estuary is chesapeake Bay. In one sense, it is a long, narrow arm of the Atlantic Ocean that reaches northward into Maryland. Although it is only 190 miles (306 km) long, it has a 7,200 mile (11,585 km) shoreline. More than 150 rivers feed into it, including the Susquehanna and Potomac.

Salt Water Wetlands

Salt marshes border many of our nation's bays and estuaries. Grasses are the dominant vegetation. The water level in these marshes rises and falls with the tides. The marshes form where water current is weak and where the bottom mud is fertile. The fibrous foots of the first grasses bind the muds together and encourage the spread of the marsh.

Too many people think of wetlands as wastelands. Nothing could be farther from the truth. Our salt marshes serve as a natural water purification system. They filter sediment and other pollutants out of the water that later enters the estuaries. Even more, the marsh grasses form a food base on which many marsh and estuarine animals such as clams, oysters, crabs and fish depend. One scientist has estimated that just one acre of salt marsh is worth $100,000 per year in pollution control and in wildlife service.

Chapter 5
Your Atmosphere's Environment

The unpolluted atmosphere forms a gaseous envelope around our planet. It is composed largely of nitrogen (79 percent), oxygen (20 percent), and carbon dioxide (.03 percent). Oxygen is a gas that all organisms need for survival. (You better keep breathing!).

Scientists believe the Earth arose as a hot mass of melted rock about five billion years ago. Temperatures were above 8000 degrees Celsius (14,576 Fahrenheit). As this rock gradually cooled, nitrogen and carbon dioxide were released. They formed the early atmosphere. When plants began to carry on photosynthesis, oxygen was added.

Water vapor varies from zero percent in dry air to 4 percent in very humid air. Dust particles may be present. In fact, after the 1991 volcanic eruption of Mount Pinatubo in the Philippines, dust clouds which formed were so thick that they temporarily blotted out the sun, moon and stars!

Scientists recognize several distinct layers of the atmosphere. The layer immediately above the Earth's surface is the troposphere (TROW-poe-sfear). It extends to a height of about 10 miles (16.1 km). In the troposphere, temperatures decreased with altitude.

You should have a pretty good idea what weather is. After all, you have to either put up with it or welcome it almost every day of your life! Weather is made up of precipitation (water), wind, air pressure, clouds and humidity.

The weatherman on TV describes weather–the changes that occur from one day to the next. The term climate describes weather in a given region, like your state, over a period of years. Almost all the weather or climate events take place in the troposphere. Moisture is present in the troposphere as a gas, known as water vapor. When there is more moisture in the air than it can hold, small water droplets are formed. A cloud is formed when these tiny droplets come very close together but do not touch. When they flow together and come in contact with each other, a drop of rain is formed.

The Water Cycle

Clouds form from evaporating water (1) and eventually turn into rain clouds (2). Precipitation–rain and snow (3)–falls to the Earth and runs off the surface (4), infiltrating into the soil (5). The water percolates through the soil into the groundwater (6) and layers of deep rock (7). Evaporation occurs when precipitation falls from the clouds (8). Water also evaporates from plants (9) streams and rivers (10), soil (11), and the lakes and oceans (12), eventually forming clouds (1).

Major types of clouds are stratus, cumulus, cirrus, and nimbus. Cirrus clouds appear in layers or smooth sheets. Cumulus clouds look like piled up cotton. Cirrus clouds are delicate curved wisps high in the sky. The dark gray clouds seen during thunderstorms are called nimbus.

Immediately above the troposphere is the stratosphere (STRAT-toe-sfear). It is between 10 (16.1 km) and 30 (48 km) miles above the Earth. In the stratosphere, the temperature remains constant at lower levels. But at higher levels, the stratosphere gradually warms up the about 28 degrees Fahrenheit (-3 degrees Celsius). The absorption of ultraviolet (short wave) light from the sun by ozone causes this warming.

Cloud Types

Cirrus clouds (1) are isolated, feathery, and are arranged in bands. Cirrostratus clouds (2) appear as a thin, whitish veil. Cirrocumulus clouds (3) form puffy white balls and thin wisps. Altostratus clouds (4) are thick, gray veils. Altocumulus clouds look like dense, fleecy balls. Stratocumulus clouds (6) are soft and gray-looking and often cover most of the sky. Nimbostratus clouds (7) are thick, dark, and shapeless. Stratus clouds (8) look like flat, white sheets.

Layers of Atmosphere

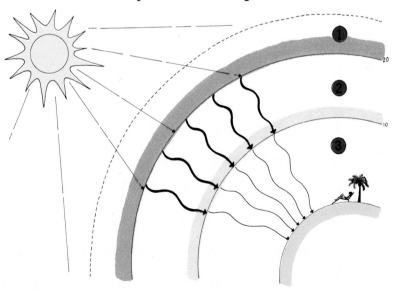

The ionosphere–20+ miles (1), the stratosphere–10-20 miles (2), and the troposphere–0-10 miles (3). The ozone shield is found in the lower part of the stratosphere.

A swallowtail butterfly. Swallowtails can be found worldwide, but they are becoming rare because their food plants are being destroyed by herbicides and by bog drainage.

Animals of the Air

The only animals that can fly are insects, birds and bats. Scientists have identified about 800,00 kinds of insects. Perhaps five million kinds remain to be discovered! Insects are found in almost every type of biome. Only in the oceans are they scarce.

Well-known American insects include dragon flies, may flies, grasshoppers, katydids, bedbugs, aphids, moths, butterflies, flies, ants, mosquitos, fleas, beetles, bees, wasps, and hornets. The rate of wing beat ranges from four per second in large butterflies to 1,000 times per second in small relatives of the house fly called midges.

Several insects, like butterflies and locusts, make long flights. Some painted lady butterflies migrate between California and the Hawaiian Islands. The monarch butterfly makes an annual migration between the northern states and Texas. Some locusts migrate in huge swarms numbering billions. These "living clouds" often black out the sun.

There are more than 9,000 kinds of kinds on this Earth. They are found in every biome. Some are well-known because they are brightly colored, such as the bluebird, cardinal, oriole and goldfinch.

Some are game birds like the grouse, quail and pheasant. Many kinds are valuable because they eat weed seeds (tree sparrow) or harmful insects (warblers, woodpeckers and wrens).

The rate of wing beat ranges from four per second in herons to 75 beats per second in hummingbirds. The fastest birds in North America are the golden eagle (160 mph [257 km/hr]) and the peregrine falcon (180 mph [290 km/hr]). The Arctic Tern has the largest annual migration–a round trip of 20,000 miles (32,180 km) between its sub-Arctic breeding grounds and its winter home in Antarctica.

Bats are widely distributed. Only in the Arctic and Antarctic are they absent. Most of the more than 900 species live in the tropics. The United States and Canada are home to at least 90 kinds of bats.

Bats perform valuable services to humans. They consume many destructive insect pests. Farmers have used bat waste, called guano (GWAH-no), as fertilizer for centuries. Some bats pollinate the plants on which they feed. The largest bats, known as flying foxes. have a wing span of over five feet (1.5 m). Vampire bats live in Central and South America. They prey mainly on cattle–taking about one teaspoonful of blood every day. Some bats can catch fish with their claws as they swoop low over the surface of a pond or stream. Several bat species that live in the United States, like the brown bat, hoary bat and red bat, migrate south as cold weather comes.

The common vampire bat. Vampire bats can be found all over South America.

The Journey of a Nitrogen Atom

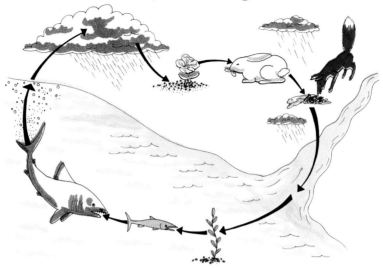

As the nitrogen atom journeys from water to plants to animals,
it links all the major environments–air, water, and land.

How Your Environments are Tied Together

We have learned about land, water, and atmospheric environments almost as it they are completely separate from each other. This is not true. They are tied together by elements that move from one environment to another in a circular manner. Let's follow a nitrogen atom (N) through such a cycle.

The N atom (as nitrate-NO3) is washed from the atmosphere during a thunderstorm. Later it is taken up from the soil by a buttercup growing on the bank of a river. A rabbit feeds on the buttercup, and then is eaten by a fox. The N atom moved from the buttercup into the rabbit and was left in the remains the fox did not eat. The remains are washed into a stream by heavy rain. As the carcass decays, the N atom is released into the water (as nitrate-NO3).

The N atom is carried through an estuary and then into the sea. Here it moves through a marine food chain. It is absorbed by a tiny green plant which is then eaten by a herring. Then the herring is eaten by a shark. The N atom (as part of a large molecule) passes out of the shark with its body wastes. These wastes are then acted on by bacteria which eventually releases the N atom (as nitrogen gas-N2).

It bubbles up to the ocean surface, then escapes into the atmosphere from which it originally came. The N atom has completed one full turn of its cycle. And in the process, all the major environments–land, water, and air– were tied together.

Why We Should Take Care of Our Environments

Over a period of millions of years, every organism on Earth–from tiny crustaceans to the mighty whales–have adapted to live successfully in a particular environment. When we pollute or destroy parts of these environments, we make the organisms' struggle to survive much more difficult. In some cases, we may even cause its extinction. It is important for all of us to do our best to preserve the health of our environments. Then we can help promote the health of all life on planet Earth.

Abyss–the deepest part of the ocean, characterized by darkness and near-freezing temperatures.

Barrier island–a narrow island that forms parts of an island chain off the Atlantic and Gulf Coasts.

Biomes–the largest land community in a given region that is easily recognizable by a biologist.

Carbon dioxide–a gas that normally forms less than one percent of the Earth's atmosphere.

Continental shelf–a shelf-like extension of a continent into the shallow part of the ocean.

Climate–long-term record of temperature, precipitation, wind velocity and relative humidity in a given region.

Community–the total number of organisms living in a given area.

Coniferous tree–a cone-bearing tree like a spruce, fir or pine.

Coral reef–a sub-marine formation of limestone largely composed of the skeletons of coral animals.

Deciduous tree–a tree that loses its leaves in autumn, such as the oak, maple or elm.

Ecology–the study of the inter-relationships between organisms and their environment.

Ecosphere–that region of the Earth which is occupied by living organisms.

Ecosystem–any part of the world of nature in which there are interactions between organisms and their living and non-living environment.

Environment–the total "world" outside the body of an organism.

Glacial lake–a lake formed by the melt waters of a glacier.

Grassland biome–biomes that are dominated by grasses, such as the prairies of North America.

Great Barrier Reef–the largest coral formation in the world, located off the coast of Australia.

Insect larvae–immature stage of an insect.

Krill–tiny crustaceans that live in the ocean; serve as food for large whales.

Ozone–an abundant atmospheric gas in the stratosphere that protects organisms from ultra-violet light.

Population–the total number of individuals of a species in a given area.

Ptarmigan–a grouse-like bird common in the tundra biome.

Tropical rainforest–the biome which develops in that part of the tropics which has at least 80 inches (200 cm) of annual rainfall.

Troposphere–the layer of atmosphere that extends from the Earth's surface to a height of about 10 miles (16 km).

Tundra–the Arctic grassland biome located between the coniferous forests and the lands of permanent ice and snow.

Weather–the record of temperature, precipitation, relative humidity and wind velocity over a short period such as a day, month or year.

Wetlands–fresh or salt water communities that normally are flooded with water most of the year.

The Biomes

The purpose of this project is to focus on the location of the world's biomes and the changes (good or bad) that humans have caused.

Obtain and outline map of the world from your teacher or librarian. (You can also draw one yourself!) Show the location of all the biomes discussed in this book. You can get more information from other Target Earth Earthmobile books or references in your school or public library.

Ask your parents how many of these biomes you have visited. How often did you visit a particular biome? Which of the biomes was the most interesting to you? Why? Have humans changed the original condition of these biomes? If so, in what way? Were these changes harmful to plants and animals? Were they beneficial to some? Hand in your completed project, with your biome map, to your teacher.

Animals of the Land Environment–Ants

The purpose of this project is to learn about the behavior of ants–movements, food getting, and fighting.

Find a colony of large ants near your school or home. Put a very tiny dab of water color on three ants with a sharp-pointed brush. Give each ant a distinctive color. The following day, come back to the colony and observe it for one hour. Follow the movements and actions of the marked ants. How many minutes did each marked ant spend above ground? Underground? How often did each ant emerge?

After leaving the ant mound, do the marked ants all follow the same trail? Does a single ant use different trails? How far does each marked ant move from the ant mound after each emergence? Did you see any of the marked ants fighting? If so, did they fight with each other or with other insects? Did any of the marked ants gather food? Could you identify the food?

Make a sketch of the trails used by the marked ants. Show their length. If you own a camera, take a close-up picture of the ant mound and the ants you have studied. Hand in your report to your teacher, with your trail sketch and pictures.

Animals of the Land Environment–Insects

The purpose of this project is to develop skill in identifying insects and to learn about their behavior.

Find a large wild plant growing in your school yard, around your home, in the park, or on a friend's farm. Suggested plants are goldenrod, milkweed, wild daisy, day lilies, honeysuckle, or even a young tree.

Examine the plant carefully for insects. Observe for one hour. With the help of an insect guide, do your best to identify the insects. If you can't, then identify them by using letters A, B, C, D, etc. Record the total number of insects of each kind that you saw on the plant. Take notes on the appearance of each kind of insect–size, shape, color, piercing (teeth-like) or chewing mouth parts.

Where did you find the insect–on leaves, stems, branches, or flowers? At what height was each insect found? What was the insect doing? Was it loafing, feeding, fighting, mating, or laying eggs? Was it moving? If so, in what direction–up, down, toward the inside of the plant, or toward the outer part?

If you have a camera, take a picture of the plant and some insects. Include all the data in a report and hand it in to your teacher.

Animals of the Water Environment–Tadpole

The purpose of this project is to study the metamorphosis of a frog.

With the aid of a small net, collect some small tadpoles from the shallow water at the edge of a pond or weedy lake. Also gather some of the green scum floating in the water, and several buckets of pond water. Bring the samples back to school.

Put sand and gravel in the bottom of the aquarium. Add a few large rocks and a few branches. Gently add the pond water to the aquarium until it is about two-thirds full. Keep the aquarium out of direct sunlight. Water temperature should be a constant 70 degrees Fahrenheit. Keep a thermometer in the water.

Now add the algae and the tadpoles. The tadpoles. The tadpoles will feed in the algae and rest in the shallow water over the rocks. Add some underwater plants like Elodea, which you can get from any pet store. Keep an accurate record of the metamorphoses of the tadpoles into frogs. Record the day on which each of the following takes place:

(1) appearance of gills, (2) disappearance of gills, (3) appearance of hind legs,
(4) appearance of front legs, (5) shortening of the tail, (6) gulping of air at the surface of
the water, (7) tadpole rests partly out of the water, (8) tadpole has changed into a frog.

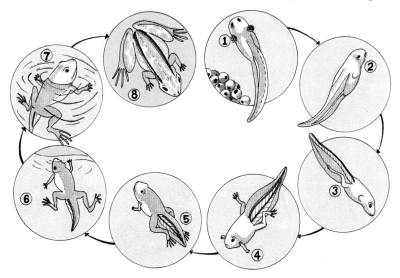

If you have a camera, take pictures of the tadpoles at different stages of development. Hand in a report on your project to your teacher. Return the frogs to the pond.

Animals of the Air–Birds

The purpose of this project is:

- to develop skills in identifying birds
- to become familiar with flight corridors
- to determine the functions of bird flight

The best time for this study of bird flight zones is in April and May. Find an area near your school or home that has a high bird population. Equip yourself with a pair of binoculars and a bird guide. Visit your selected study area early in the morning about one hour after sunrise. If you have a camera, take a picture of your study area. Your study should last one hour.

Observe the birds in flight. Try to identify species with the aid of a field guide. (Perhaps you can have an experienced bird-watcher help you.) The following species are common in much of the United States:

- English sparrow
- cardinal
- robin
- red-headed woodpecker
- house wren
- rock dove or pigeon
- European starling

If you cannot identify the species, designate the kind on bird using the letters A, B, Show C, D, etc. Estimate both the height and distance of each flight you observe. Show on a data sheet (such as the one below) whether the flight path was 0 to 15 feet (4.5 m), 15 to 30 feet (4.5 to 9 m), 30 feet (9 m) to 45 feet (13.5 m) or above 45 feet (13.5 m). Do your best to figure out the purpose of each flight:

- flight to a song perch
- food gathering
- defense of territory
- escape from predators

- escape from humans
- search for a mate
- search for a nesting site
- search for nesting materials (string, feathers, dried grass, sticks, etc.)

After recording your data, figure out the preferred flight zone for each species you observed.

Sample Data Sheet

Flight distance	0-10 yards (0-9m)	10-50 yards (9m-45m)	50-100 yards (45m-90m)	100+ yards (90m+)
Height Zone Above 45 feet (13.5m)	E	C	A, Wren	F
30-45 feet (9m-13.5m)	A, B, B	Blue jay		
15-30 feet (4.5m-9m)	Sparrow	E	D	
0-15 feet (0m-4.5m)	Sparrow	C		

Index

A

abyss–26, 27
acorns–13
Africa–14,16,22
air–6, 8, 17, 22, 31, 36
air pressure–31
Alaska–18, 23
Alberta–24
algae–21
Amazon River–18
America–20
anchovy–26
Antarctica–35
Antarctic Ocean–25
antelope–14
ants–6, 34
aphids–34
Aransas Wildlife Refuge–24
Arctic–10, 23, 35
Arctic Ocean–25
Arizona–9, 14, 20
Asia–11, 14, 16, 22
Atlantic–24, 25, 27, 28, 30
Atlantic City (NJ)–28
atmosphere–31, 36
Australia–14, 28
autumn–13, 22

B

bacteria–6, 36
badger–14
barrier islands–28
basin–25
bass–23
bats–18, 34, 35
beaches–28
bears–5

beaver–24
bedbugs–34
beech–9
bees–34
beetles–12, 34
biome–9, 12, 13, 16, 34
birches–10
birds–6, 7, 10, 12, 14, 18,
    23, 24, 28, 34
black bear–13
blackflies–10
blood–8, 35
blueberries–23
bluebird–34
bluegill–23
boating–19
bogs–23
Brazil–18
breeding–13, 19, 35
budworms–12
buffalo–14
buffalo grass–13
bullhead–23
bulrush–23
burrows–16
bush–18
buttercups–36
butterflies–6, 18, 34

C

cactus–9, 16
California–9, 14, 20, 34
Canada–23, 35
canyons–27
Cape Cod–28
Cape Hatteras–28
carbon dioxide–17, 31

cardinal–34
caribou–10, 11
carnivore–12, 14
carp–22, 23
catfish–22
cat-tail–23
cattle–14, 35
Central America–16, 35
cheetah–14
chemicals–23
Chesapeake Bay–30
chestnuts–13
Chile–14
chipmunk–12, 13
cirrus clouds–23
clams–30
climate–9, 17, 19, 21, 25, 31
Clinton, Bill–25
clouds–31, 32
cod–26
cold-blooded–10
Colorado River–20
community–5, 6, 9
Coney Island–28
coniferous forest–10, 13
continental shelf–26
coral animals–28
coral reef–28
corn–13
Costa Rica–18
coyote–14
crabs–30
cranberries–23
cranes–24
Crater Lake–20
crayfish–22
creosote bush–16

crowberry–10
crustaceans–22, 24, 37
cumulus clouds–32
currents–25, 28

D
Dakotas–24
dams–20
deciduous forest–12
deer–13, 18
deerflies–10
desert–9, 14, 16
dragonfly–22, 34
drought–13, 16
drugs–17
ducks–24
dust–31

E
eagle–13, 23, 35
Earth–8, 10, 17, 19, 22, 25, 31, 32, 34, 37
earthworms–6
ecosphere–5, 8
ecosystem–5, 6, 7, 22
eels–23
egret–23, 24
Egyptians–22
electricity–20
elements–36
elephants–26
elk–12
elm–6
endangered species–23
environment–5, 8, 23, 36, 37
erosion–14, 17, 28
estuaries–30
Europe–11, 13
evergreen–11
extinctin–37

F
falcon–35
farmer–35
farming–13, 17, 20
fertilizer–22, 35

fir–11
fish–25, 26, 27, 28, 30, 35
fisheries–19
fishing–19, 21, 22, 23
fleas–34
flies–34
floods–14, 22, 23
Florida–27, 28
flowers–6, 16, 22
food chain–36
forest–9-13, 16, 23
foxes–10, 12, 13, 16, 36
frogs–10, 24
frost–21

G
garbage–7
gas–31
geese–24
generator–20
gila monster–16
giraffe–14
glacier–9, 20, 22
Glacier National Park–5
Gobi Desert–14
goldfinch–34
grama grass–13
grass–7, 10, 28, 30
grasshoppers–6, 14, 34
grasslands–13, 14, 23
greasewood–16
Great Barrier Reef–28
Great Lakes–20, 23
Great Plains–23
grizzly bear–12
grouse–34
guano–35
Gulf Coast–24
Gulf of Mexico–28
Gulf Stream–25
gulls–23

H
habitat–17, 19, 23
halibut–26
Hawaii–34
hawks–13, 23

hemoglobin–8
herbivores–10, 11, 13, 14, 16
heron–23, 24, 35
herring–26, 36
hickory–13
hickory nuts–13
hookworms–7
Hoover Dam–20
hornets–34
hotsprings–23
huckleberry–10
humidity–31
hummingbird–35
hunting–19

I
ice–9
Idaho–14
Indian Ocean–25
insects–6, 7, 10, 12, 18, 22, 28, 34
Iowa–24
iron–8
island–18

J
jackrabbit–14, 16

K
kangeroo rat–16
Kansas–9
katydids–34

L
Lake Mead–20
Lake Michigan–21
lakes–10, 19-21, 23
land–9, 36
landscape–9
lark–14
larvae–22
leaves–7, 13, 22
lemmings–10
leopard–14
lion–14

lizards–10, 18
locusts–34
logging–13
loon–23
lynx–12

M

mackerel–26
Maine–9, 28
mammals–10
Manitoba–24
maple–9, 13
maple seeds–13
marshes–23, 24, 28
Maryland–30
Massachusets–28
mayfly–22, 34
mesquite–16
Mexico–14
Miami Beach–28
mice–6, 7, 10, 12, 14, 16,
    18, 22
midges–34
migration–10, 12, 23, 26,
    28, 35
minerals–8
mining–13
mink–23, 24
Minneapolis–5
Minnesota–20, 24
minnows–22
Mississippi River–13, 22
Missouri River–22
mollusks–28
monkey–18
moon–31
moose–11
mosquitos–6, 10, 34
moss–10
moth–18, 34
mountains–27
mule deer–12
muskellunge–23
muskox–10
muskrat–24

N

National Wildlife
    Refuge–24
nesting–13, 24
Nevada–14, 20
New Jersey–28
New Mexico–14
New York–28
nimbus clouds–32
nitrogen–31, 36
North America–11, 13, 22,
    24, 35
North Carolina–28
nutrients–26
nuts–22

O

oak–6, 13, 28
ocean–23, 24, 28, 30, 34, 36
ocean bottom–26, 27
ocelot–18
Ohio–9
Ohio River–22
omnivore–13
opossum–13
Oregon–14, 20
organism–8, 9, 16, 21, 22,
    25, 26, 37
oriole–34
otter–23, 24
owl–13, 16
oxygen–7, 8, 21, 22, 25,
    26, 31
oysters–30
ozone–32

P

Pacific–23, 25, 26
parasites–7
parrots–18
perch–23
perma-frost–10
pheasant–34
Philippines–31
photosynthesis–21, 22,
    26, 31

pigment–8
pigs–7, 13, 16
pike–23
Pinatubo, Mount–31
pine–11, 28
plains–27
planets–8, 25, 31
plants–7, 10, 13, 21, 23,
    25, 36
plateaus–27
poison ivy–6
pollution–23, 30, 37
pond–10, 35
population–5
porcupine–12
porpoises–26
Potomac River–30
prairie–9, 13
prairie dogs–14
precipitation–31
pronghorn antelope–14
Puerto Rico–13

Q

quail–34

R

rabbit–6, 10, 13, 18, 36
raccoon–13, 23
rain–31, 36
rainbow darter–22
rainfall–10, 12, 13, 14,
    16, 25
rainforest–16-18
rancher–14
raspberries–13
rat–7, 18
rattlesnake–16
red snapper–26
reindeer–10
reservoir–20
ridges–27
rivers–19-22, 30
robin–6
Rocky Mountains–13
roots–13, 30

roses–6
roundworms–7

S

Sahara Desert–14
salmon–22, 23, 26
salt–25
salt marsh–30
saltwater–30
sand dollars–28
sand dunes–28
sand flats–28
sardines–26
Saskatchewan–24
scythebill–18
sea anemones–28
sea cows–26
sea otter–26
sea shells–28
seals–26
sedges–10
sediment–23, 26, 30
seeds–22
shad–23
shallows–23, 26, 28, 30
sharks–26, 36
shrews–13
shrubs–7
Sierra Mountains–13
smelt–23
snails–24
snakes–10, 18
snow–9, 11
snowy owl–10
soil–6, 8, 9, 13, 17, 23, 36
South America–16, 18, 22, 35
soybeans–13
sparrow–34
Spain–27
spawn–23
spider–18
spring–12, 22
spruce–11, 23
squirrel–12, 13
star fish–28

stars–31
stems–22
Stone Age–22
stratified–21
stratosphere–32
stratus clouds–32
streams–22, 23, 25, 35, 36
sturgeon–22
sub-soil–10
summer–10, 12, 16
sun–8, 10, 31, 32, 34
Susquehanna River–30
swamps–23
swans–24
swimming–19

T

tadpoles–22
tamarack–23
tapeworms–7
temperature–8, 12, 16, 21, 23, 31, 32
terns–23, 35
Texas–14, 24, 28, 34
threatened species–23
thrush–12
thunderstorms–16, 32, 36
ticks–6
tides–30
timber wolf–12
toxic–23
trees–6, 7, 13, 16
tropics–13, 16, 17, 18, 28
troposphere–31, 32
trout–22, 23
tulips–6
tuna–26
tundra–9, 10, 23
turtles–22, 23

U

ultraviolet–32
United States–13, 14, 16, 18, 22, 24, 28, 35
Utah–14

V

vapor–31
vegetation–10, 13, 28, 30
venom–18
vines–18
viper–18
volcano–20, 31

W

walleye–23
walrus–26
warbler–12, 34
wasp–34
water–6, 8, 9, 13, 17, 20-22, 23, 24, 25, 26, 30, 31, 36
waterfleas–22
waterfowl–10, 24
waterlilies–21
water pressure–26
waves–28
weather–10, 31
weeds–22
wetlands–19, 23, 24, 30
whales–26, 37
wheat–7, 13
White House–25
wildlife–17, 23, 24
wild rice–23
willows–10
wind–17, 28, 31
winter–10, 12, 24
Wisconsin–20
wolves–10
woodpecker–12, 16, 34
worms–22
wren–34

Y

Yellowstone National Park–23

Z

zebra–14

TARGET **E**ARTH™ **C**OMMITMENT

At Target, we're committed to the environment. We show this commitment not only through our own internal efforts but also through the programs we sponsor in the communities where we do business.

Our commitment to children and the environment began when we became the Founding International Sponsor for Kids for Saving Earth, a non-profit environmental organization for kids. We helped launch the program in 1989 and supported its growth to three-quarters of a million club members in just three years.

Our commitment to children's environmental education led to the development of an environmental curriculum called Target Earth™, aimed at getting kids involved in their education and in their world.

In addition, we worked with Abdo & Daughters Publishing to develop the Target Earth™ Earthmobile, an environmental science library on wheels that can be used in libraries, or rolled from classroom to classroom.

Target believes that the children are our future and the future of our planet. Through education, they will save the world!

Minneapolis-based Target Stores is an upscale discount department store chain of 500 stores in 33 states coast-to-coast, and is the largest division of Dayton Hudson Corporation, one of the nation's leading retailers.